Meow!
Will you answer
the call for adventure?

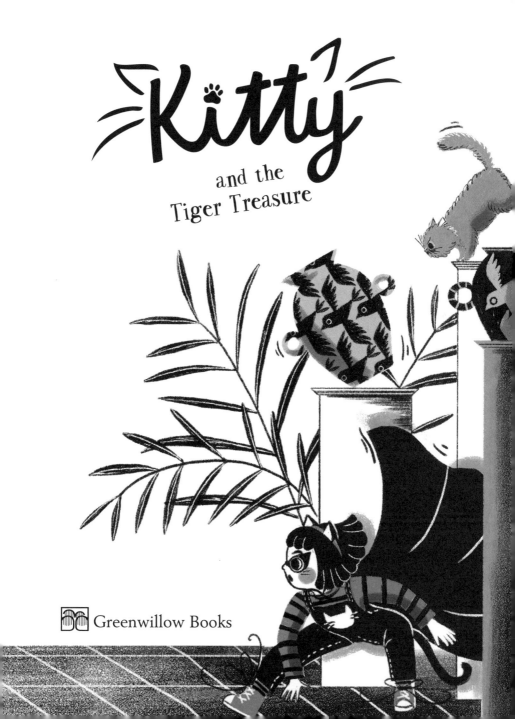

Kitty

and the
Tiger Treasure

Greenwillow Books

For Inky, the most mischievous cat in town–P. H.

For Helena and her cat crew–J. L.

Kitty and the Tiger Treasure. Text copyright © 2019 by Paula Harrison
Illustrations copyright © 2019 by Jenny Løvlie
First published in the United Kingdom in 2019 by Oxford University Press; first published in the United States by Greenwillow Books, 2019

www.harpercollinschildrens.com.

The text of this book is set in Berling LT Std.

Library of Congress Control Number: 2019944594

ISBN 9780062934765 (hardcover) — ISBN 9780062934741 (paperback)
19 20 21 22 23 PC/LSCC 10 9 8 7 6 5 4 3 2 1
First Edition
 Greenwillow Books

Contents

Meet Kitty & Her Cat Crew

Kitty

Kitty has special powers—but is she ready to be a superhero just like her mom?

Luckily, Kitty's cat crew has faith in her and shows Kitty the hero that lies within.

Pumpkin

A stray ginger kitten who is utterly devoted to Kitty.

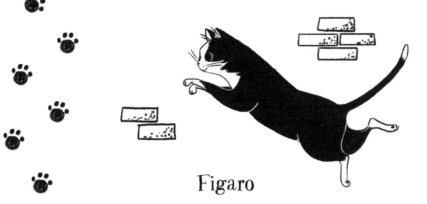

Figaro

Wise and kind, Figaro knows the neighborhood like the back of his paw.

Pixie

Pixie has a nose for trouble and whiskers for mischief!

Katsumi

Sleek and sophisticated, Katsumi is quick to call Kitty at the first sign of trouble.

Kitty

and the
Tiger Treasure

Chapter 1

Kitty sprang from the sofa to the door in a single bound. "Stop right there!" She pointed her finger at Pumpkin the cat. "You won't get away with it this time!"

Pumpkin, a roly-poly ginger kitten

with black whiskers, scampered out of reach. "Can't catch me!" he meowed, darting into Kitty's bedroom.

Kitty chased after him, giggling. Pumpkin leaped onto the bed and rolled over to let Kitty tickle his fluffy tummy.

Kitty's mom came in. "What are you two up to? There's a lot of giggling going on in here."

"We're playing Catch the Bandit!" Kitty told her. "It's a new game we invented, and it helps me improve my superpowers."

"I see!" Mom smoothed back Kitty's dark hair. "I'm glad you're practicing, but it's getting late. It's time to settle down and go to bed."

Kitty climbed under her blanket. "I am very sleepy."

"I'm not surprised!" Mom smiled as she tucked Kitty in.

Kitty smiled back. She knew her mom understood how important it was to practice her powers. Kitty's family had a special secret. Mom was a real superhero and went out at night to use her catlike abilities to help people. Kitty and her little brother, Max, had the same superpowers as their mom. Kitty could see in the dark and hear noises from far away. She could also balance perfectly and perform amazing somersaults. Best of all, she could talk to animals!

A few weeks before, Kitty had been on her very first nighttime adventure. She had met Pumpkin, who had no place to stay. Kitty was so happy the kitten had come home with her. Now he was part of the family, and he slept on Kitty's bed every night.

"Don't forget we've got a big day tomorrow," added Mom as she tidied Kitty's clothes. "We're going to the Hallam City Museum to see the new exhibit. The Golden Tiger statue will be there, along with lots of other ancient treasures."

Kitty sat up in bed again. "Is the Golden Tiger really covered with diamonds?"

"That's right! And it has large eyes made of emeralds," Mom told her.

"I can't wait to see it!" cried Kitty.

"I'm glad you're excited," said Mom, laughing. "Sleep well, honey!"

Kitty turned on her night-light and snuggled down under the covers. She couldn't wait for tomorrow. The new treasures at the museum were supposed to be amazing. The Golden Tiger statue was decorated with dozens of jewels. Kitty couldn't wait to see them all winking and glittering!

Pumpkin padded across the bed and flopped down beside her. His eyes shined in the dim light, and his fur was velvety soft against Kitty's arm. Kitty sighed and closed her eyes. Pictures of imaginary treasure floated around in her head.

Pumpkin wriggled. "Kitty, are you asleep?" he whispered.

Kitty's eyes opened. "Not yet! What's wrong, Pumpkin?"

The kitten's whiskers twitched. "What's the Golden Tiger statue like? Is it enormous?"

"It looks small in the pictures. It's probably no bigger than you!" Kitty smiled.

"Then why is it so special?" asked Pumpkin.

"Mom says it was buried in an ancient tomb for thousands of years before archaeologists found it. It's made of gold and covered in diamonds. The tiger's eyes are made from sparkling emeralds."

"It must be valuable, then." Pumpkin snuggled against Kitty's shoulder.

"It's priceless!" Kitty told him. "And it could be magical, too. The legend says that the Golden Tiger listens to your heart's desire, and if you touch its paw, it will grant your greatest wish."

Pumpkin's eyes widened.

"Dad told me all about it," continued Kitty. "Lots of people have had good luck after seeing the statue, but there's a curse, too. If a bad person does something to make the statue angry, it will conjure up ghostly spirits to seek revenge!"

Pumpkin shivered. "Ooh—spooky!"

"I hope I can get close enough to see it tomorrow. The exhibit is opening for the first time, so I think the museum will be crowded."

"I wish I could come with you!" said Pumpkin. "Are cats allowed to visit?"

Kitty shook her head. "I don't think so." She lay quietly for a moment. Then she sat up so suddenly that she nearly knocked Pumpkin off the bed. "I've got a great idea! If we visit the museum *tonight*, then you'll be able to see everything and there will be no crowds at all. We'll have the whole place to ourselves!"

Pumpkin's nose twitched. "But . . . is

the museum very scary?"

"It's full of interesting things. We can look at them together." Kitty tickled Pumpkin under the chin. She knew the kitten got nervous about new things and new places. After all, he'd been all alone before he met Kitty. "Don't you think it would be fun to have a new adventure?"

Pumpkin nodded slowly. "I like the sound of the statue with the diamonds and emeralds. Jewels are so sparkly, aren't they?"

Kitty nodded, pushed back the covers, and jumped out of bed. "We should go right now! The museum is only ten minutes away, and I can use my superpowers to find a way across the rooftops."

Pumpkin sprang onto the window seat and pushed back the curtain with his nose.

A crescent
moon shined brightly, and
light poured into the room. Kitty
felt excitement bubble inside her. She
gazed at the roofs of the houses all laid
out in long rows. She could see a way
through the chimneys as if it was a
secret path only she knew!

Pumpkin twitched his nose again. "I just hope it doesn't rain."

"If it does, I'm sure we'll find somewhere to shelter." Kitty took out her superhero clothes and tied on her black cape and cat tail. Finally she added her cat ears and looked in the mirror. Dressed in her cat costume, she felt like a real superhero! Her powers lit up inside her like the moon coming out from behind a cloud.

When she opened the window, the night wind blew in and the curtains flapped. Kitty climbed onto the ledge, her heart skipping. Going out to see the museum's treasures was exciting, and also a tiny bit scary. "Are you ready, Pumpkin? It's time to start our next adventure!"

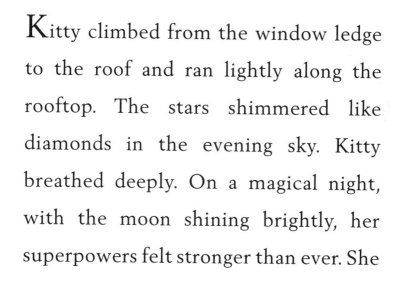

Chapter 2

Kitty climbed from the window ledge to the roof and ran lightly along the rooftop. The stars shimmered like diamonds in the evening sky. Kitty breathed deeply. On a magical night, with the moon shining brightly, her superpowers felt stronger than ever. She turned a cartwheel, feeling her powers tingling through her body.

"Do you know the way to the museum, Kitty?" asked Pumpkin, climbing up beside her.

Kitty looked over the rooftops, her special night vision sharpening. "Yes, I'm sure I do. Look, there it is, on Crown Street." She pointed to a tall building made of pale stone. It had a domed roof and huge columns on each side of the front door.

Pumpkin and Kitty ran along the roof and around a chimney. Kitty's cape flew out behind her as she leaped from one house to the next. The wind swirled around, making the trees sway, and the shadows of the branches danced in the moonlight.

Suddenly, a sleek black cat with a white face and paws stepped out from behind a chimney. Kitty recognized her friend Figaro right away. "Hello, Figaro!

What are you doing here?"

"Waiting for you, of course!"
Figaro twirled his whiskers. "I
spied you climbing out your

window and I thought to myself, what sort of adventure will Kitty embark on tonight?"

"We're going to the museum to see the Golden Tiger statue," explained Kitty.

"We want to see it before the crowds come tomorrow." Pumpkin waved his tail excitedly.

"The statue of the Golden Tiger is a rare and mysterious object!" Figaro's eyes gleamed. "I have heard the strange legends about its powers."

"Would you like to come with us?" asked Kitty.

"I would be delighted, dear Kitty." Figaro bowed his head. "Lead the way!"

Kitty led them across the rooftops to Crown Street. The museum roof was flat, with a glassy dome in the middle. The building was enormous, with doors and windows on every side.

"I wonder where the Golden Tiger statue will be." Kitty clambered down to the nearest ledge and peered through a window. There was a row of ancient

swords inside a glass cabinet.
She climbed to the next window
and saw china vases and

silver plates inside the display cases.

Pumpkin stayed close to Kitty while Figaro stepped gracefully from ledge to ledge. Kitty peered into each dark room. The museum was so vast. Where would the Golden Tiger be? At last she spotted a shiny banner: COME SEE THE ANCIENT TREASURES OF THE INCA WORLD! Following the arrow, she leaped to the next window ledge and looked eagerly inside.

The Golden Tiger stood on a small platform surrounded by a red velvet rope. A spotlight shined directly onto the statue, and the tiger's emerald eyes glowed so brightly that for a moment Kitty wondered if it was alive. The Golden Tiger was sitting upright with one paw raised in the air. It was gold with elegant black stripes across its back and a coat encrusted with diamonds.

"Wow!" cried Pumpkin. "It looks amazing."

"I must say it's very impressive." Figaro swished his tail. "Very impressive indeed!"

Kitty pressed her nose to the window.

The shelves around the statue were full of treasures, but the Golden Tiger was the shiniest and most amazing one of all. "I'd love to get a bit closer," said Kitty. "Then I could find out whether the statue really does grant a wish when you touch its paw!"

"What would you wish for, Kitty?" asked Pumpkin.

"I don't know!" Kitty bit her lip. "Those jewels look so beautiful. I'd love some diamonds, emeralds, and rubies of my own!"

Pumpkin rubbed his head against Kitty's knee fondly.

"I believe a closer inspection of the statue is an excellent idea," said Figaro. "I can think of many things I would wish for: some pampering at the beauty salon, or a four-course meal at Sinclair's Finest Fish restaurant! Let us go inside at once."

Kitty hesitated. "Do you really think we should? No one's supposed to go in there at night."

"Please, Kitty!" Pumpkin turned his big eyes on her.

Kitty nodded. "All right—but we must be really careful. Look, there's a way in over there!" She took hold of a drainpipe, ready to climb to the ledge below.

There was a whooshing noise overhead.

"*MEEOOOW!*" A creature landed heavily on Kitty's shoulder.

Kitty wobbled, grabbing the drainpipe to keep her balance. Pumpkin panicked and leaped onto Kitty's foot, pinning it to the ledge with his paws. "Eek! Don't worry, I've got you!"

The creature, a gray Persian cat with bright eyes, sprang onto the ledge and stared up at Kitty fiercely. "You won't get away with this!" she hissed. "I know a cat burglar when I see one. You've come to steal from the museum, haven't you? Well, I won't let you!"

Kitty stared back in surprise. Who was this new cat and why did she think they were thieves?

Chapter 3

The gray cat flicked her tail crossly. "I'm the museum cat, and I won't let anyone get away with stealing." She glanced at Figaro and Pumpkin. "And you two should be ashamed of yourselves for helping her. No honest cat would do such a thing!"

Figaro's sleek black-and-white fur bristled. "How dare you accuse us of being common thieves?"

"Hush, Figaro! It's all right." Kitty turned to the gray cat. "You don't need to worry. We're not here to steal anything. We only came to look at the Golden Tiger statue because we were so excited to see it. My name's Kitty, and I have superpowers. These are my friends Pumpkin and Figaro."

"Oh, yes, I've heard about you." The

gray cat studied Kitty's cape and cat ears. Then she bowed her head. "My name's Cleo. I'm sorry I jumped on you."

"You should be *very* sorry!" Figaro scowled deeply. "Imagine landing on someone like that! It's hardly civilized."

"I got the wrong idea when I saw you sneaking along the window ledge," said Cleo. "I hope I didn't frighten you all."

"Don't worry—we're fine!" Kitty told the cat. "I suppose we must have looked a bit suspicious."

Figaro made a *humph* sound and turned away to clean his paws.

Pumpkin crept along the ledge to look at Cleo with curious eyes. "Do you really live here in the museum?"

"I sleep in an office at the back of the

building," explained Cleo. "It belongs to Stan, the night guard, but he's fallen asleep in his chair again. So it's up to me to keep the museum safe. There are a lot more precious things here now that the new exhibit has arrived."

"It sounds like *you* should be the museum's official guard," Kitty told her.

Cleo rubbed her ear with her paw. "I'd love to be a real guard, but the humans don't seem to notice how hard I work. I adore living here—it's amazing! Would

you like me to show you around?"

"Yes, please!" Kitty's eyes shined. "And we'd love to look at the Golden Tiger."

"It's a very special statue," said Cleo proudly. "It looks even better up close. I'll take you inside—just make sure you don't touch anything."

"What's that funny shadow over the Golden Tiger?" Pumpkin asked suddenly. "I can hardly see the statue anymore."

Kitty peered through the window.

Pumpkin was right. There was a shadow there . . . and it was moving!

"It looks so spooky!" squeaked Pumpkin. "It's not the curse, is it?"

Kitty pressed her face close to the window. The shadow slipped around the side of the display cabinets and disappeared. Then something, or someone, cut the power to the lights. Suddenly the whole room plunged into darkness.

A tingle ran down Kitty's back. "What's going on? Cleo, something's happening!"

Cleo darted over at once. Figaro stopped cleaning his paws and joined them.

The moon broke
from behind a cloud, sending
a shaft of light through the dome
window. The shadow became clearer.
It had a furry brown-and-white
coat and long, floppy ears.

"That looks like a springer
spaniel. What's a dog doing

in the museum?" gasped Kitty.

"An intruder!" Cleo's fur stood on end. "And I was so busy talking that I didn't even notice."

The dog moved stealthily around the gallery until it stood right beside the Golden Tiger.

"Paws and whiskers!" exclaimed Figaro. "It's heading straight for the statue."

They watched in alarm as the dog leaned closer and reached out his paw. . . .

"STOP THIEF!" cried Cleo. "That doesn't belong to you!"

The dog knocked the statue from its pedestal. The Golden Tiger rolled across the museum floor, its diamonds sparkling in the moonlight. The statue's emerald eyes glowed like the eyes of a real tiger. Then the dog picked up the statue in his jaws and ran off into the shadows.

"He's getting away!" squeaked Pumpkin.

Kitty saw the desperate look on Cleo's face. "Don't worry! We'll help you catch him." She shimmied down the drainpipe to the ledge.

The she threw up the window and

leaped inside. The museum was silent and still.

Cleo shook her head. "Stan must

have forgotten to set the burglar alarm again!"

Kitty looked around and shivered. The last time she'd visited the museum, the whole place had been bright and noisy and full of people.

Now there was a shadowy shape in the corner, and moonlight glinted on something shiny. Kitty caught her breath. Then her eyes sharpened, and she saw a wax model of a soldier carrying a spear. She breathed slowly to calm her racing heart. The thief was somewhere in the building, and she was determined to catch him.

Cleo and Pumpkin tumbled into the room behind her. Figaro climbed in last, with a flick of his tail.

"Cleo, can you take us to the exhibit room?" said Kitty.

"This way!" Cleo led them up a grand marble staircase into a splendid gallery beneath the domed ceiling. Moonlight shined through the window above. All around them, the treasures of the exhibit were arranged in beautiful cases.

There were fans painted in delicate colors, ancient coins, and silver plates studded with rubies.

A spotlight shined down on the space where the Golden Tiger had been. Cleo paced around the empty pedestal, her tail swishing. "I should have noticed!" she muttered. "I should have been watching more carefully."

Kitty's heart sank. The best treasure of all was missing, and everyone in Hallam City would be disappointed. Worst of all, what if the statue really *did* grant wishes? If bad guys got hold of the Golden Tiger, they might wish for something terrible!

"Look—paw prints!" Pumpkin pointed at the prints leading away into the dark.

They followed the paw prints, but the trail ended at the stairway.

"I fear the trail has gone cold," said Figaro. "This building is enormous. We have little hope of finding the scoundrel now."

"Wait, listen!" Kitty focused with her super hearing. She picked up the sound of paws padding on the floor above.

52

"He's upstairs! We can still catch him."

Her heart thumped as she rushed toward the staircase. The race to stop the thief was just beginning!

Chapter 4

Kitty ran lightly up the spiral stairs, and the cats dashed after her. Cleo's eyes narrowed when the group reached the top. Her gray tail swayed worriedly as she searched the shadowy room.

Kitty heard a creaking sound. "This way!" she whispered.

At the far end of the gallery, the dog was opening the window with his nose. Kitty crept nearer, her orange sneakers silent on the polished floor. The robber had put the statue down. Maybe, if they got close enough, they could snatch the Golden Tiger back.

Pumpkin's tail brushed against a display, knocking over a pile of old coins. They jangled as they rolled around and around in circles. The dog whirled

around, and the moonlight gleamed on his patchy coat. His eyes were wide, and he had a strange, faraway look, like someone daydreaming.

Kitty shrank into the shadows, raising a finger to her lips. Pumpkin looked like he was about to meow, but Figaro clapped a paw over his mouth. The thief gave a low bark before picking up the statue, pushing the window open, and squeezing through. Kitty raced to the window and looked along the wide ledge, but the dog had already vanished.

Slipping outside, Kitty clambered to the roof. With her super night vision, she scanned the shadowy streets. Cleo and the other cats scrambled up beside her. Pumpkin twitched his whiskers nervously. Moonlight poured down, reflecting off the museum's glassy dome.

Cleo meowed impatiently. "How could I have been so silly! If I'd been paying attention instead of chatting with all of you, then this would never have happened."

"It's not your fault!" Kitty spotted the dog running down an alleyway. The Golden Tiger gleamed in his jaws. "Look, there he is!" Scrambling to the edge, she got herself ready to leap across to the opposite roof.

"Be careful, Kitty!" called Pumpkin.

Kitty felt her superpowers tingling, and her heart skipped with excitement. She was determined not to lose sight of the robber dog. She sprang to the next house and kept on running, her feet barely touching the roof.

Using her outstretched arms to balance, she leaped from one house to the next. Her cape flew out behind her, as black as midnight. The ground looked far away, but she wasn't afraid. She trusted her superpowers. She could do this!

The springer spaniel reached a row of shops. Kitty edged closer, ducking behind a chimney when the dog glanced around. A moment later, he disappeared from view. Cleo and Pumpkin scampered over to Kitty.

"Where did he go?" whispered Pumpkin.

Figaro puffed a little as he caught up. "He's obviously a slippery sort of dog. He could be anywhere!"

Kitty crept to the corner of the building and found a metal staircase. "We can use this fire escape to get down." She tiptoed down the steps, and the cats followed her.

The robber dog was hurrying down the street, the statue still clamped in his jaws. He stopped beside a shop, pushed the door open, and went inside.

Kitty followed him. She stared up

THE HAPPY PAWS PET SHOP

at the store sign, which was lit by a streetlamp. "The Happy Paws Pet Shop," she read aloud. "Do you think he lives here?"

Pumpkin's eyes were wide. "Maybe he's stealing for his owner."

"Very odd!" said Figaro. "I haven't heard much about this pet shop. I think it only opened a few months ago."

Cleo sighed. Her gray fur was tinged with orange in the glow of the streetlight. "I should have done a better job. I wasn't watching the museum carefully enough. I have to fix this!"

"You *were* doing a good job," Kitty told her. "Let's check the windows and find the best way to get inside."

"Great idea! If we can take the thief by surprise—" Cleo fell silent as the door opened again.

The robber dog darted outside, his eyes wide and glazed. He scampered down the street and vanished into the dark.

"He doesn't have the statue anymore," said Kitty. "He must have left it inside!"

"There's a way in over there." Figaro pointed to an open window.

"You and Pumpkin should stand guard, ready to warn us if the thief returns," said Cleo. "He may be a dangerous kind of dog."

"Very well!" Figaro nodded. "Be careful, won't you?"

"Don't worry—we will!" Kitty scaled the side of the shop and peered through the window.

It was dark inside, and there was a great deal of shuffling and squeaking as the animals moved about inside their cages. Kitty slipped through the window. Then she climbed onto a cupboard and dropped soundlessly to the floor, helping Cleo down after her.

Moonlight reflected off the gray tiled floor. The shop was filled with dozens of cages—tall bird pens, guinea pig and rabbit hutches, and tortoise cages. Toward the back, shelves of pet food and bedding were hidden in darkness.

"Where do you think he left the treasure?" whispered Kitty.

Cleo sniffed the air. "It's difficult to follow his scent. There are too many different animal smells in here."

"Then we'll just have to search."

TIGER
TREATS

TIGER
TREATS

Kitty looked around for possible hiding places. She pointed to the shop counter. "I'll look over here." But as she turned, she got the strange feeling that someone was watching her.

Kitty saw a pair of dazzling golden eyes studying her from behind the pet food shelves. Kitty's night vision grew sharper, and she knew at once that they were cat's eyes. Jewels winked on the cat's collar.

Kitty caught her breath. Who was this new cat and what did it know about the snatching of the Golden Tiger?

Chapter 5

The cat with the golden eyes stared back at Kitty. Then it vanished, without a word, through a doorway into a back room.

"Did you see that?" whispered Kitty. "We should ask that cat what it knows about the statue." She turned to Cleo, but the gray cat was gone.

Kitty hesitated. Had Cleo been scared away by the other cat? Or did she have a plan?

A light came on in the back room. Kitty hurried along the rows of cages. She passed hutches full of sleeping bunnies, and wide-awake hamsters running in their wheels. Two parrots with beautiful green and red feathers were perched in a tall cage with their heads under their wings.

Kitty stopped in the office doorway.
Piles of shiny objects covered the desk,
the chair, and the filing cabinets inside.

Every corner of the room was filled with glittering treasures—silver plates, strings of pearls, and jewels in every color of the rainbow.

Kitty gaped. All these treasures must be stolen! Was the robber dog really doing all this?

"Purr-fect greetings!" trilled a high voice.

Kitty jumped. The cat with the golden eyes lay on a pile of shiny coins. She had orange fur, and the name PRECIOUS was spelled out on her collar in diamonds. Her pointed ears pricked up as Kitty approached. There was an odd look in her eyes, as if she was trying to puzzle Kitty out.

"My name is Kitty!" said Kitty. "I'm looking for a tiger statue. The springer spaniel who stole it came through your door just a few minutes ago."

The cat's tail flicked to and fro. "My name is Precious. You must be the girl with superpowers who I've heard so much about. I bet your talents are very useful indeed!"

Kitty frowned. There was something strange about this cat. "I try to use my powers to help others. That's why I'm looking for the Golden Tiger statue. It was taken from the museum tonight, and it's very special! Did you see the robber dog that came in here?"

Precious began grooming herself.

"No, I didn't see a thing."

"But he came right inside!" Kitty watched Precious lick her paws and clean behind her ears. Suddenly she had a thought. What if the dog wasn't in charge of the robbery at all? Precious seemed like a sly sort of cat. She was definitely the type to organize a secret mission to steal the museum's treasure.

Kitty gave Precious a stern look. "I think you know a lot more about the statue than you've said. Tell me where it is!"

Precious laughed. "Why should I? The Golden Tiger is mine now. It makes an excellent addition to my collection. I *do* like shiny things!" She stretched out on top of the gold coins and gave an exaggerated yawn.

"But everyone's coming to see the new exhibit tomorrow!" said Kitty. "They'll be so disappointed not to see the Golden Tiger—it's a very important statue." She stopped herself from telling Precious that the statue could grant wishes. A cat like Precious might wish for something very selfish—something that hurt others!

"They'll just have to be happy with the other things in the museum," snapped Precious. "Humans are such whiny creatures! All I've taken is one *tiny* statue. Can't they manage without it?"

Kitty glared at the cat. There was no point trying to reason with her! Kitty edged forward, looking for the statue behind the pile of coins.

"Oh, don't bother trying to find

it." Precious waved her paw airily at a metal box on the wall. "I locked it away in the safe. I shall take it out later and admire the diamonds before I take a nap."

Kitty sprang over to the safe. It was shut tight, and it had a lock. Precious laughed again. Kitty swung around, asking, "Why does that dog steal things for you, anyway? Don't you both know it's wrong?"

"He does anything I say." Precious beamed. "Everyone does, once they look into my eyes . . . including you!" She met Kitty's gaze. Kitty felt the cat's golden eyes drawing her in like a magnet. Precious spoke in a growly tone. "Listen very carefully! You will forget that you ever met me. You will not remember this pet shop. You will leave now and never come here again."

Kitty's head swam. For a moment she could hardly remember why she was there. Then she thought about how much she wanted to help Cleo, and her eyes focused again. "You may have hypnotized the springer spaniel, but I don't think it works on me! Maybe it's because of my superpowers."

"Huh!" Precious flounced down from the coin pile and turned her back on Kitty, settling herself on a velvet blanket.

Kitty thought quickly. It was obvious that Precious was much more dangerous than she'd first thought. If no one stopped the golden-eyed cat, she could make the dog steal more and more treasure. She might even hypnotize other animals and force them to join in.

An idea popped into Kitty's head. Maybe there was a way to use the stories about the statue! Perhaps she could scare Precious into giving back the treasure.

"There's something you don't know about the Golden Tiger," she began. "Many say that the statue has a terrible curse."

Precious stopped grooming and pricked up her ears. "Why would I care about that?"

"Because the curse says that if someone upsets the statue, it will send scary spirits to take revenge," said Kitty.

Precious was silent for a moment. "Do you think it's true?"

"I don't know." Kitty noticed the cat's tail swaying uneasily. She tried to think how to make the story more believable. "But if it *is* true, I expect the spirits come in the dead of night and creep in through tiny cracks around the doorframe." She shivered. That would be spooky if it were true!

Precious sat up straight, her tail flicking faster and faster. "Spirits? Door frames?"

There was a bang followed by a loud clatter from the front of the shop.

Kitty jumped. Maybe the curse *was* real!

"What was that?" Precious leaped across the room, grabbing Kitty's hand with both paws. "Save me, Kitty. I'm not a bad cat, really!"

"Stay close to me." Kitty's heart pounded like a drum as she crept toward the doorway. She could hear the pets squeaking and fluttering, disturbed by the strange noises. Kitty dodged as a box of treats toppled from a shelf. Then she leaped bravely though the door.

Chapter
6

A hamster ran under Kitty's legs. "Someone's opened all the cages!" she gasped. "The animals are escaping."

The little hamster climbed the shelves, cheeping sharply. Then a pink-eared rabbit hopped across the shop

90

counter. The green and red parrots flew out of their cage, squawking, "Stop, thief!"

"The curse is coming true," moaned Precious. "I wish that horrible statue had never come here."

Kitty spotted Cleo peeping out from behind a fish tank. Then the gray cat pushed a box of hamster food off the shelf. Kitty understood at once. Cleo had caused all this chaos to make

Precious believe the story about the curse. The museum cat must have been listening the whole time!

Precious ran around in circles, her pointy ears swiveling from side to side. There was another crash as Cleo knocked a stack of dog leashes to the floor. Precious arched her back fearfully. "Kitty, the spirits are here to take revenge. Oh, save me!"

Cleo ducked behind the fish tanks as the golden-eyed cat ran around in a panic.

"Why don't I take the statue back to the museum?" suggested Kitty. "That will stop the curse."

"Yes, yes! I will give you the silly statue!" cried Precious. "I never want to see it again." Running to the safe, she twisted the lock, and the door clicked open.

Kitty removed the Golden Tiger. It felt heavy in her hand. "Don't worry, you're safe now," she told Precious. "But to be really sure, you should tell the dog to return all the other stolen things."

"I promise I will," said Precious, her eyes wide.

"And never use your hypnotism on him, or anyone else, again," added Kitty.

Precious nodded eagerly. "I'll be good from now on. Please don't let the curse get me!"

"Wait for me here. I'll make sure everything's safe," Kitty told her before running back into the shop.

With Cleo's help, she ushered most of the pets back into their cages.

There was a noise at the window, and Pumpkin's face appeared. "Kitty, the dog is returning, and someone has switched a light on upstairs!" Pumpkin whispered.

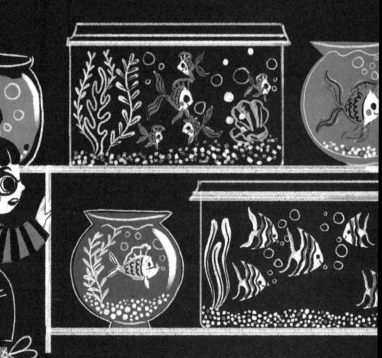

"Goodbye, Precious!" called Kitty. "Remember what you promised."

Kitty and Cleo hid in the shadows as the springer spaniel trotted into the pet shop, then darted out the back door.

Kitty held the Golden Tiger tightly. "We did it!" she whispered. "Cleo, you're the *best* guard cat a museum could ever have! You were so clever making all that noise so that Precious would worry about the curse."

CLOSED

Cleo puffed out her chest. "I could tell that cat wouldn't give the statue back easily, so I made it as noisy as possible! I couldn't have done it without you, Kitty. I wish I had someone as kind and loyal as you helping me all the time."

Pumpkin and Figaro ran over to join them, and Pumpkin eyed the statue worriedly. "I know the curse is just a story . . . but maybe we should take the Golden Tiger back to the museum as quickly as we can!"

"Well said!" Figaro yawned and

stretched. "All this excitement is exhausting. Besides, my stomach is empty and I need a nice big supper."

They climbed back up the fire escape to the roof. Running along the edge of the rooftops, they jumped from building to building. The moon rose higher in the sky and the stars glittered.

Leaping to the top of the museum, Kitty stopped for a moment to look across the city. The night wind swirled, making her cape flutter.

"Oh, no!" cried Cleo. "Stan must have

discovered that the statue is missing."

Kitty peered through the glass dome. Two men were leaning over the pedestal where the Golden Tiger had been. One was wearing a dark-blue guard

uniform. The other man had a bald head that gleamed in the moonlight.

"Who's that other man?" asked Kitty.

"That's Mr. Martinez, the head of the museum," Cleo told her.

"What do we do now?" cried Pumpkin. "We can't put the statue back without them seeing us."

Kitty frowned. "I suppose we could explain everything . . . but they might blame the owners of the pet shop for what Precious did, and this wasn't their fault at all."

Figaro twirled his jet-black whiskers.
"I may have an idea! Follow me."

They followed Figaro through an

upstairs window. Their steps echoed as they climbed down the marble staircase. Ducking behind a pillar, they watched more museum staff run toward the exhibit room.

"So many people—it feels like the whole city will be here soon." Cleo flicked her tail. "We'd better be fast!"

"This way!" Figaro scampered into the museum restaurant and stopped beside a row of mouthwatering cakes, each displayed inside a glass cake stand.

"What's your plan, Figaro?" asked Kitty.

Figaro waved his paw at a beautiful vanilla and strawberry cake with sugar frosting. "As we cannot return the statue to its rightful place, we need to put it somewhere it will be found immediately in the morning. If we place it here, people will spot it right away. I suggest using the empty chocolate cake stand."

Kitty looked along the row of cakes, past the lemon cake with the white icing. At the end was an empty stand labeled CHOCOLATE CAKE.

"You're right!" Cleo nodded approvingly at Figaro. "Many visitors and staff come to have a morning coffee and a pastry, and they'll spot the statue right away." She jumped up onto the counter and lifted the lid of the cake stand with her teeth.

Carefully, Kitty placed the Golden Tiger on the stand. Remembering the legend, she wondered if the statue knew her heart's desire. She touched its paw, and for a second the tiger's emerald eyes glowed in the dim light. Kitty smiled to herself and a tingle ran down her spine.

Cleo replaced the lid. "Quickly! We mustn't be found here."

Kitty paused for a moment as the others darted back to the corridor. Finding a pencil behind the counter, she scribbled a message on a waiter's pad:

Here is the Golden Tiger, which was stolen but returned safely—thanks to Cleo, the museum cat.

Smiling, she left the piece of paper beside the statue and ran to join the others.

By the time they reached the rooftop, the clock tower was chiming midnight.

"Thank you all so much." Cleo bowed deeply. "Kitty, I will never forget the help you gave me. You are a true friend!"

"I'll come and visit you when my mom and dad bring me to the museum," promised Kitty. "They'll love the story of how we saved the statue!"

Kitty, Pumpkin, and Figaro made their

way home across the rooftops in the moonlight. Pumpkin brushed against Kitty's legs. "Kitty, did you touch the Golden Tiger's paw?"

Kitty smiled at the kitten. "Yes I did! Just before I left it on the cake stand."

Pumpkin skipped around a chimney. "What's your greatest wish? Do you think it will come true?"

"*My* greatest wish would be for a delicious slice of salmon cooked in a herb sauce," Figaro put in.

"I thought I'd wish for rubies and diamonds, but my wish wasn't for me— it was for Cleo. I hope the museum is grateful for everything she's done, and they make her an official guard." Kitty stopped to look at the beautiful night sky and the city lights winking in the darkness. Then she looked at Figaro and Pumpkin. "Anyway, I have my greatest wish already. Being here with my friends is the best adventure in the world!"

Super Facts About Cats

Super Speed

Have you ever seen a cat make a quick escape from a dog? If so, you know they can move *really* fast—up to thirty miles per hour!

Super Hearing

Cats have an incredible sense of hearing and can swivel their ears to pinpoint even the tiniest of sounds.

Super Reflexes

Have you ever heard the saying, "Cats always land on their feet"? People say this because cats have amazing reflexes. If a cat

is falling, it can quickly sense how
to move its body into the right position
to land safely.

Super Vision

Cats have amazing nighttime vision. Their
incredible ability to see in low light allows
them to hunt for prey when it's dark outside.

Super Smell

Cats have a very powerful sense of smell.
Did you know that the pattern of ridges on
each cat's nose is as unique as a human's
fingerprints?

Have you read Kitty's first adventure?

Kitty's family has a secret. Her mom is a hero with catlike superpowers, and Kitty knows that one day she'll have special powers and the chance to use them, too. That day comes sooner than expected, when a friendly black cat named Figaro comes to Kitty's bedroom window to ask for help. But the world at night is a scary place—is Kitty brave enough to step out into the darkness for a thrilling moonlight adventure?